MERRY CHRISTMAS, HOOPER DOOPER

Story and pictures by Bijou Le Tord

Random House/New York

MERRY CHRISTMAS, HOOPER DOOPER

"Hooper Dooper, wake up. Tonight is Christmas Eve."

"We have to leave now, Hooper, if we want to find a
Christmas tree in the forest."

"Xip, xip, xip?"

"Yes, Hooper. The forest will be beautiful, covered with
new snow."

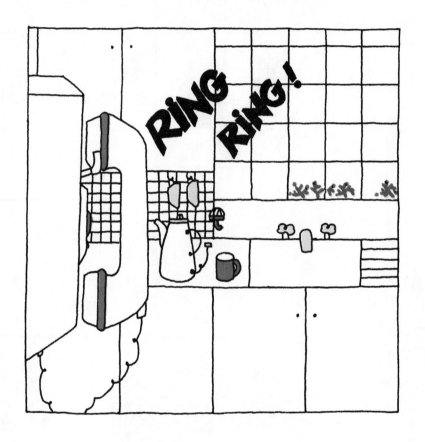

RING RING, RING RING!

"Hello. Yes, this is Brother Long John. Is that you, Little Will?
You'll be here early tonight? And Big Nannie, too? Fine."

"Brother Long John, remember to pick a good tree.
Not too little and not too big. All right, have a nice day."

"Xip, xipxip, xip?"

"That's right, Hooper, you'll need your snow tires. Hurry, Dooper!"

"Xoop!"

"Look, Hooper! This is where the best
Christmas trees in the country grow."

"Xip, xipxip?"

"Of course, we'll find the right size tree, Hooper."

"Now, this is a fine tree. Bright green needles, well-trimmed branches."

"Xipxipxip, xip?"

"Yup, a bit too tall!"

"Perhaps you'd like this one, Hooper? Handsome, full, shiny?"

"Xip, xip."

"Ah! It is too wide."

"And, this pretty young fellow. Is he too small?"

"Xipxip, xip xip!"

"Hmm. Next year, he'll be just right."

"Oh, poor scraggly tree. The winds hurt him."
"Xiiiip!"
"So many trees, Hooper. And we still have none."

"Now it is time to go back, Hooper."

"Xoop, xoop, xoop, xiip!"

"I know. I'm very unhappy, too."

"Christmas does not feel right without a tree."

"Xooop. Xip, xipxip!"

"Oh . . . you have an idea, Hooper?"

"What kind of an idea? Where are you going?
Hooper, come back! HOOPER!"

Tracktracktrack.

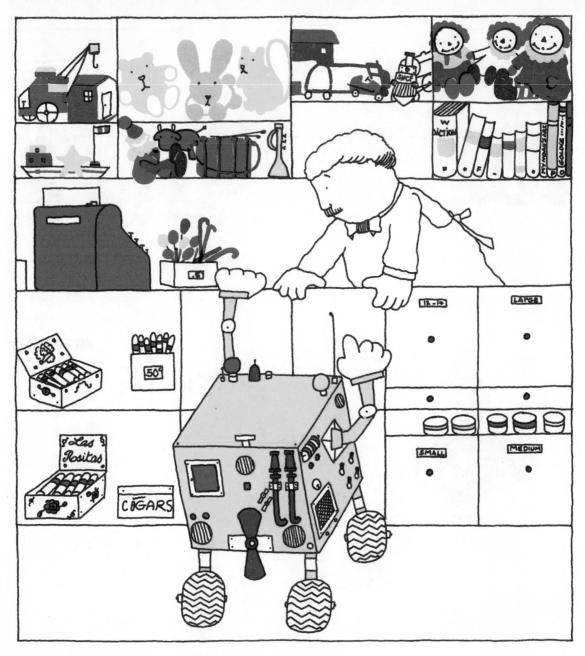

"And a star for your tree, Hooper."

"Xip xip xip, xip."

"Thank you. You too. I know you'll have a nice Christmas."

Tracktracktrack.

"Xipxip!"

"Big Nannie! Little Will! I'm glad you are here.
But Hooper isn't back."

"Brother Long John, I'm not a detective,
but I see Hooper's fresh tire-tracks in the snow."

"Do you see Hooper anywhere, Little Will?"
"No, sir!"

"Big Nannie, Hooper is nowhere."
"Nowhere?"
"Nowhere at all!"

"Someone is knocking at the door!"

"HOOPER IS HOME, my friends! LOOK!"

"Xipxip."

"OOOH!"

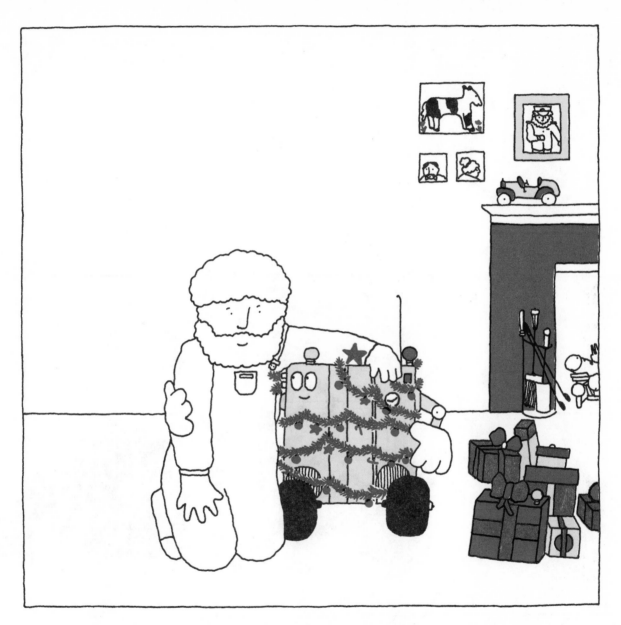

"My, Hooper . . . you are the most beautiful Christmas tree
I have ever seen."

"O Christmas tree, O Christmas tree,
how lovely are thy branches. . . ."

"Christmas is a quiet time for friends to feel warm and happy together."

"Oh, look. Hooper is asleep."

"MERRY CHRISTMAS, HOOPER DOOPER."